The MEGAMOGS
and the
dangerous doughnut

For Jack

A Red Fox Book

Published by Random House Children's Books
20 Vauxhall Bridge Road, London SW1V 2SA

A division of The Random House Group Ltd
London Melbourne Sydney Auckland
Johannesburg and agencies throughout the world

1 3 5 7 9 10 8 6 4 2

First published in Great Britain by The Bodley Head Children's Books 1996

Red Fox edition 2000

Printed in Hong Kong by Midas Printing Ltd

THE RANDOM HOUSE GROUP Limited Reg. No. 954009
www.randomhouse.co.uk

ISBN 0-09-953951-9

The MEGAMOGS
and the
dangerous doughnut

PETER HASWELL

Glitzy Mitzy · Sardine Sid · Phil Fleacollar · Fishpaste Fred · Derek Dogbender

RED FOX

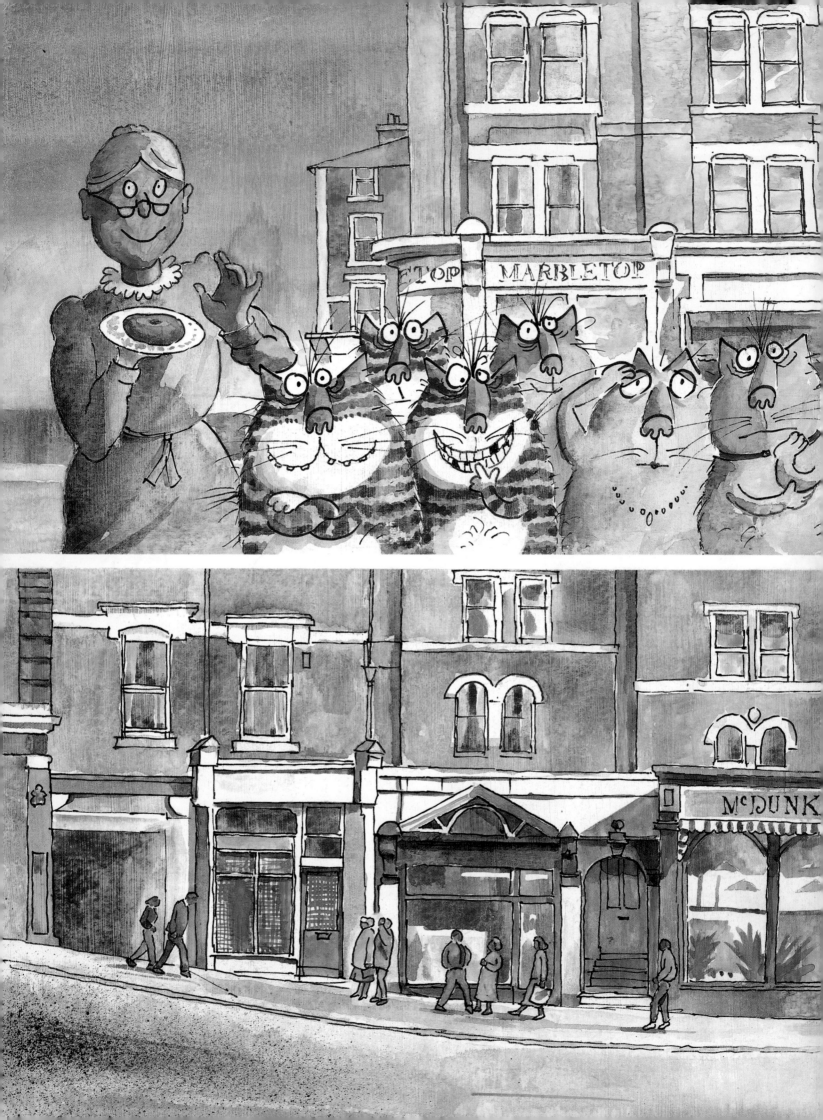

In a quaint old shop at the top of a High Street, a quaint old lady called Miss Marbletop sold Marbletop's Dainty Doughnuts. She also kept a mighty, mind-boggling mob of scatty, tatty, batty-brained mogs. They were called Miss Marbletop's Megamogs.

One morning, Duncan McDunk opened a rival shop at the bottom of the High Street selling McDunk's Deadly Doughnuts.

Miss Marbletop was mad. 'There's only room for one doughnut shop in this town,' she muttered. 'McDunk will have to go.'

But then disaster struck…

Out of the blue, Miss Marbletop was called away to care for her sick sister. 'I'm doomed,' she wailed as she boarded the train. 'The dreaded McDunk will collar my customers. I'll be forced to shut up shop!' Then the whistle blew and the train pulled out of the station taking Miss Marbletop with it.

Kevin Catflap, Captain of the Megamogs, frowned. 'That McDunk,' he said. 'What a skunk! Right then, we've got to beat him and save Miss M. So no lazing, lounging or fat-cat scrounging. No roof-top posing or tin can nosing. We've got serious work to do.'

'What's the plan, Kev?' asked Tracy Tinopener.

'We're going to run the shop and keep the customers coming,' said Kevin. 'So no creeping away and sleeping all day. Come on you cats – let's get back and SERVE!'

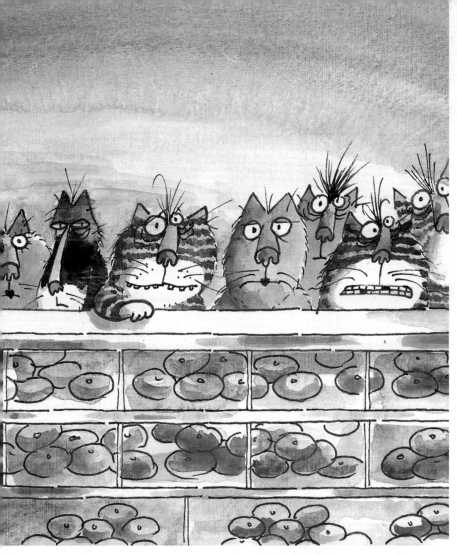

The Megamogs went back to the shop. They stood. They waited. They wilted. They sighed. They sagged. But not a single customer came through the door all day.

'It's no good,' said Derek Dogbender. 'We might as well chuck it in.'

'Face it, Kev,' added Glitzy Mitzy. 'McDunk's done for us.'

'Keep your hair on,' said Kevin. 'McDunk is obviously up to something and I want to know what it is. So tomorrow we're going to find out.'

'What are we going to do, Kev?' asked Gary Gristle.

'I'm not saying yet,' replied Kevin. 'But it's going to be SNEAKY!'

Next day, the Megamogs put on disguises.

Then they sneaked, snukked, sidled and slunk down the High Street to spy on McDunk. And this is what they saw…

McDunk had strung up a banner and people were piling into his shop.

BUY McDUNK'S DEADLY DOUGHNUTS
THE BEST DOUGHNUTS
IN TOWN!

Seeing the Megamogs, McDunk rushed out and shook his fist.

'Your daft disguises don't fool me, Megamogs,' he shouted. 'Hoppit! Scoot! Skidaddle – you barmy bunch of creepy cats!'

'Right,' growled Kevin as the Megamogs beat a retreat. 'We'll show that punk McDunk! We're going to get Miss Marbletop's customers back. And that means no lazing round with fizzy drinks or sneaking off for forty winks. No yapping, scrapping or catnapping. We're going to do something.'

'What can we do, Kev?' asked Fishpaste Fred.

'I'm not saying yet,' said Kevin. 'But I'll tell you one thing. It's going to be LOUD!'

Next day, the Megamogs got out their musical instruments.

Then they climbed into Miss Marbletop's racy red sports car, drove down to McDunk's and delivered a musical message to the people.

'*Buy Marbletop's Dainty Doughnuts*,' sang Glitzy Mitzy and Tracy Tinopener. '*The best doughnuts in the country…doo-doo scoobie-doo!*'

McDunk dashed out of his shop and shook his fist in fury.

'You can cut the commercial, you crummy cats!' he bellowed. 'It won't work!'

But it did.

The crowds deserted McDunk's and dashed back up to Miss Marbletop's shop.

RBLETOP

'Aha!' snorted Kevin, smugly. 'We did it. We diddled McDunk!' But he was wrong. Next morning, as they were preparing to open the shop, the Megamogs heard a great booming, blasting and blaring outside.

'There's something going on out there, Kev,' said Fishpaste Fred. 'And I don't like the sound of it!' The Megamogs went out to look.

McDunk was packing people into a bus to drive them down to his shop.

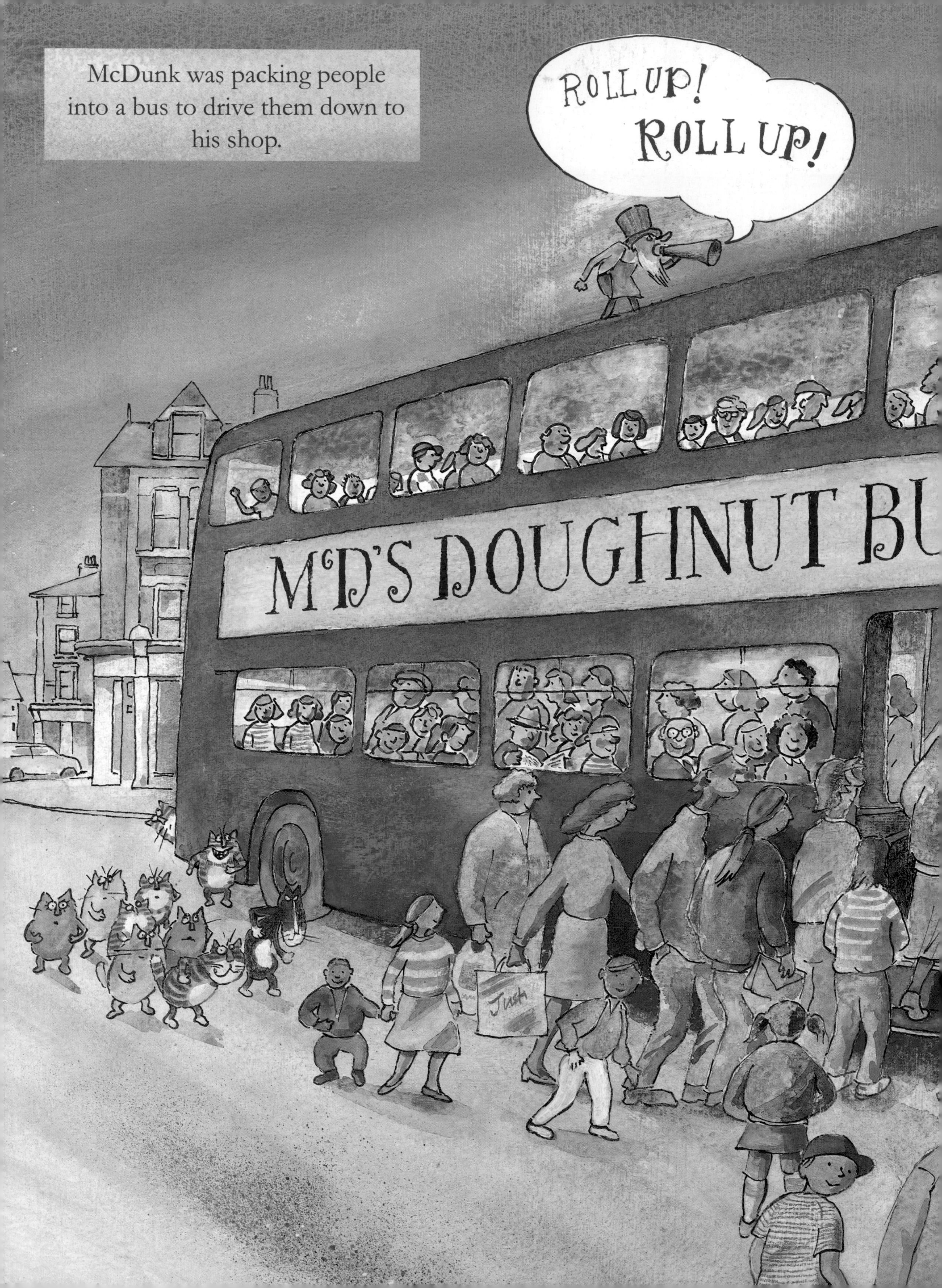

'*Roll up!*' he was bawling. '*Come down to McDunk's for the best doughnuts in the High Street!*' Then, when McDunk saw the Megamogs, he bellowed, 'You mangy mogs! You moggie mugs! You can't beat McDunk!'

'That does it!' snapped Kevin. 'This time he's gone too far.'

Then he stepped forward.

'McDunk!' shouted Kevin. 'I'm challenging you to a Great Doughnut Contest. The loser leaves town immediately. Right?'

'Right!' retorted McDunk. 'We'll meet tomorrow. Doughnuts at dawn. And the devil take the hindmost!'

Kevin turned back to the Megamogs. 'Now,' he growled. 'Tonight there'll be no going out on the town. So…

'…no rocking, raving or mis-behaving. No jazzing, snazzing or razmatazzing. No disco bashing, party crashing, preening, prancing, sweet romancing, strutting your stuff or dirty dancing. Because tomorrow we've got things to do. And we're going to start EARLY.

'So pull on your pinnies,
pop on your chefs' hats and pick
up your rolling pins…

'…no dodging, dozing, ducking or diving. No shirking, lurking, skulking or skiving. Because we're going to make a doughnut that will finally flatten McDunk. And guess what?'

'What?' asked Sardine Sid.

'It's going,' said Kevin, grimly, 'to be BIG!'

Dawn. The day of The Great Doughnut Contest.

McDunk stepped into the street with a tray of his most deadly doughnuts.

'Catflap!' he yelled. 'Come out you flea-bitten bag of fluff!'

Nothing moved. The street was deserted.

Then there was a noise. McDunk looked puzzled.

The noise grew louder. And, suddenly, McDunk saw it.

'Snakes alive!' he gawped. 'It's impossible! It's unbelievable! It's BIG!'

This is what McDunk saw... ➡

It was not just a big doughnut.
It was the biggest doughnut
in history!

'Captain to ground,' said Kevin Catflap. 'Am lowering the doughnut. Over.'

'Ground to Captain,' replied Barry Binliner. 'The doughnut has landed. Over.'

'Captain to ground,' commanded Kevin Catflap. 'Aim doughnut…and let her roll. Over.'

'Ground to Captain,' reported Barry Binliner. 'The doughnut is rolling. Over and out.'

The biggest doughnut in history rolled down the High Street. Then, as it gathered speed, it became the most dangerous doughnut in history. McDunk turned and fled. He fled down the High Street. He fled out of town.

'Great!' said Kevin Catflap. 'Nice Doughnut Contest. But today's the day Miss Marbletop gets back. So nobody takes a rest. There'll be no lounging round and feet-up lazing. No sitting back and telly gazing. Because now we've got work to do.'

'Work?' frowned Glitzy Mitzy. 'Oh no, Kev – not more work!'

'We're going to make Miss Marbletop a "Welcome Home" doughnut,' said Kevin. 'And guess what?'

'Don't tell me,' groaned Fishpaste Fred. 'It's going to be BIG.'

'Worse than that,' winced Phil Fleacollar. 'It's going to be DANGEROUS.'

'No,' gloated Kevin Catflap. 'It's going to be…